MR. MESSY

by Roger Hargreaves

PSS!

PRICE STERN SLOAN

An Imprint of Penguin Group (USA) Inc.

Mr. Messy was the messiest person you've ever met in your whole life.

He looked messy because he was messy, in everything he did.

You could always tell where Mr. Messy had been because he left a trail of messy fingerprints wherever he'd been.

Oh, yes, Mr. Messy was messy by name, and messy by nature!

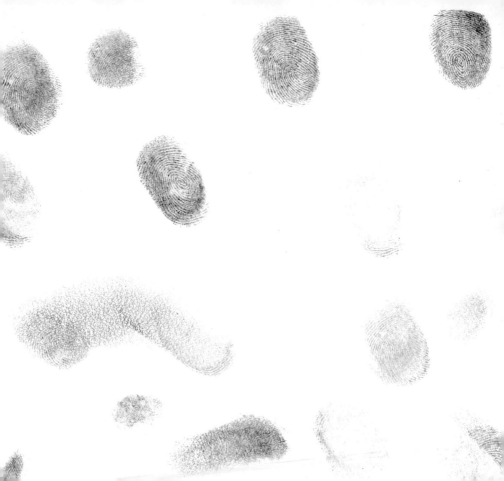

Mr. Messy lived in a particularly messy-looking house.

The paint was peeling.

The windows were broken.

There were tiles missing from the roof.

The flower beds were overgrown with weeds.

The garden gate was off its hinges.

And had Mr. Messy cut the grass in his yard lately?

He had not!

One morning, Mr. Messy woke up in his messy bed, yawned, scratched, got up, brushed his teeth (leaving the top off the toothpaste), had his breakfast (spilling cornflakes all over the floor), and then set out for a walk (tripping over a broom he'd left lying in the yard two weeks before).

There was a forest behind Mr. Messy's messy house with the messy yard, and that's where he went for his walk.

It was a particularly large forest with lots and lots of trees and it took Mr. Messy a long time to walk through it. But he didn't really mind because he felt like walking that morning.

So he walked and walked right through the forest until he came to the other side.

And do you know what he found on the other side of the forest?

Mr. Messy found the neatest, prettiest-looking little cottage that he had ever seen.

It had a lovely little yard with a stream running through the middle of it.

There was a man in the yard, clipping the hedge.

He looked up as Mr. Messy approached.

"Good morning! I'm Mr. Messy!" said Mr. Messy.

"I can see that," replied the man, looking him up and down. "I'm Mr. Tidy."

"And I'm Mr. Neat," said another man, appearing out of the house.

"Tidy and Neat," said Mr. Tidy.

"Neat and Tidy," said Mr. Neat.

"We're in business together," explained Mr. Tidy. "And the people who own this house have asked us to do some work for them."

"What sort of work?" asked Mr. Messy.

"Oh, we make things nice and neat," said Mr. Neat.

"Tidy things up," added Mr. Tidy.

"Perhaps we could come along and do some work for you?" said Mr. Neat looking at Mr. Messy, who was looking even messier than usual that particular morning.

"But I don't want things neat and tidy," said Mr. Messy looking downright miserable at the thought of it.

"Nonsense!" said Mr. Tidy.

"Fiddlesticks!" said Mr. Neat.

"But," said Mr. Messy.

"Come along," said Mr. Neat.

"Off we go," said Mr. Tidy.

"But, but . . ." said Mr. Messy.

"But nothing," said Mr. Neat, and—bundling him into their van, which was parked behind the house—off they went to Mr. Messy's house on the other side of the forest.

"Good heavens!" said Mr. Neat when he saw where Mr. Messy lived.

"Good gracious me," added Mr. Tidy.

"This is the messiest house I have ever seen in all my born days," they both said together at the same time.

"Better do something about it," said Mr. Neat.

And before Mr. Messy could open his mouth, the two of them were rushing here and there around Mr. Messy's house.

Mr. Neat hoed

and mowed

and pruned

and snipped

and clipped

and cleared

and dug

and made the yard look neater than it had ever
looked before.

Mr. Tidy cleaned

and primed

and rubbed

and painted

and mended

and made the outside of Mr. Messy's house look tidier than it had ever looked before.

Then they both went inside the house.

"Good heavens!" said Mr. Neat for the second time that morning.

"Good gracious me!" said Mr. Tidy for the second time that morning.

And then they set about cleaning the house from top to bottom.

They brushed and swept and polished and scrubbed and made the inside of the house look neater and tidier than it had ever looked before.

"There we are," said Mr. Tidy.

"All finished," said Mr. Neat.

"Tidy and neat," said Mr. Tidy.

"Neat and tidy," said Mr. Neat.

Mr. Messy just didn't know what to say.

Then they both looked at Mr. Messy.

"Are you thinking what I'm thinking?" Mr. Neat said to Mr. Tidy.

"Precisely," replied Mr. Tidy.

"What we're both thinking," they said together to Mr. Messy, "is that you look much too messy to live in a neat and tidy house like this!"

"But . . ." said Mr. Messy.

But whatever Mr. Messy said was no use, and Mr. Neat and Mr. Tidy whisked him off to the bathroom upstairs.

It had been the messiest room in the house, but now of course it was neat as a new pin.

Then Mr. Neat got hold of one of Mr. Messy's arms, and Mr. Tidy got hold of the other arm, and they picked him up and put him right into the bath.

Mr. Messy wasn't used to having baths!

Mr. Neat and Mr. Tidy washed
                    and brushed
                    and cleaned
                    and scrubbed
                    and combed Mr. Messy
until he didn't look like Mr. Messy at all.

In fact he looked the opposite of messy!

He looked at himself in the mirror.

"You know what I'm going to have to do now?"
he asked in a rather fierce voice.

Mr. Neat and Mr. Tidy looked worried.

"What are you going to have to do?" they asked Mr. Messy.

"I'm going to have to change my name!" said Mr. Messy.

And then he chuckled.

And Mr. Neat and Mr. Tidy chuckled.

And then Mr. Messy laughed.

And Mr. Neat and Mr. Tidy laughed.

And then they all laughed together, and became the best of friends.

And that really is the end of the story, except to say that if you're a messy sort of person you might have a visit from two people.

And you know what they are called, don't you?